GIDEON ELLIOT

Carnal Spellbound

GAY COMPILATION 3

GAY HYPNOTISM EROTICA

WARNING

This book contains sexually explicit scenes and adult language. It may be considered offensive to some readers. This book is for sale to adults ONLY.

* * * * * * * * * * * * * * * * * * *

Please store your files wisely where they cannot be accessed by underage readers.

Please feel free to send me an email. Just know that these emails are filtered by my publisher. Good news is always welcome.

Gideon Elliot – **gideon_elliot@awesomeauthors.org**

About the Publisher

4Fun Publishing, a member of **BLVNP Incorporated**, 340 S. Lemon #6200, Walnut CA 91789, info@blvnp.com / legal@blvnp.com
NOTE: Due to the highly emotional reaction of some people to works of erotic fiction, any email sent to the above address that contains foul language or religious references is automatically deleted by our anti-spam software and will not be seen. All other communications are welcome.

DISCLAIMER

Please don't be stupid and kill yourself. This book is a work of FICTION. Do not try any new sexual practice that you find in this book. It is fiction and not to be confused with reality. Neither the author nor the publisher or its associates assume any responsibility for any loss, injury, death or legal consequences resulting from acting on the contents in this book. Every character in this book is over 18 years of age. The author's opinions are not to be construed as the opinions of the publisher. The material in this book is for entertainment purposes ONLY. Enjoy.

Gay Compilation 3

Carnal Spellbound

Gay Hypnotism Erotica

By: Gideon Elliot

© Gideon Elliot 2014
ISBN: 978-1-62761-361-3

TABLE OF CONTENTS

BOOK TITLES

BOOK SAMPLE

GIDEON ELLIOT

NOW

Gay Romance

NOW

"Teach me to dance," Matthew said to Barry.

They had met, as they had arranged it, at the bus stop after school. It was Friday afternoon, and they had gotten permission for Matthew to stay overnight at Barry's. They were both nearly fourteen and they were both freshmen in high school, but Barry went to St. Martin's Prep and Matthew went to Harwood, the public high.

Academically, it was just as good as St. Martin's, but St. Martin's was known for its discipline and because it catered to a very wealthy clientele. Its young men were all on track to be managers and partners and practitioners and professionals, slated to join prestige firms or hang out shingles on their own in the best neighborhoods.

Its young men! Young women did not attend St. Martin's. They went to its sister school, St. Margaret's. But boys and girls took classes together in both buildings, traversing a courtyard that connected the two buildings. Their sides extended to touch each other and enclosed the courtyard, making it an atrium.

The teachers were not nuns, but they might have been, except Miss York. She looked to everyone like she had an entirely different kind of life at home from the one she was supposed to lead at school. Everyone knew she would not be renewed once the year was over. The fact that it was her last term seemed to bring out the imp of her mischief. The boys day-dreamed and talked dirty about her and the girls imagined being like what they imagined she was like when they caressed themselves.

St. Martin's and Saint Margaret's were Tudor blond stone buildings each facing across a narrow avenue, their backs to each other across the courtyard. Old umbrageous boughs spread branches green-heavy with foliage over their streets. Touching the sides of each of the buildings were a row of nineteenth-century brownstones. You would say the schools looked like castles if you were in a good mood; and fortresses if you were having a bad day. A wrought iron gazebo swirling like a great art nouveau flower stood in the center of the courtyard.

Barry had met Brenda there clandestinely more than one dark evening after school when they both had told their parents they would be studying at the library until it closed, which was at nine p.m. weekdays. They took an extra sandwich in their lunch bags just for verisimilitude.

Their tongues clung one to the other as he petted her just-beginning breasts feeling their impossibly soft firmness with proud fingers, and she felt the metal of his incipient manhood in a palm that had an uncorrupted delicacy of touch.

It was, of course, a secret, what they did together, but not one Barry kept from Matthew. Matthew listened with envy when he boasted, but he was not envious of Barry. He envied Brenda. He longed to be where Brenda had been, limp in Barry's arms, feeling him take possession, but he knew better than to say anything, even to himself.

Matthew was a good looking kid. He felt inconsequential when he was around Barry. He liked being around Barry. But it was always frustrating. Barry gave the world an edge. Whatever they did was exciting. There was romance and chivalry in it, whatever they did, whether exploring the empty lots and rotting piers by the river, riding the subway, walking along the waterfront, combing their hair in the men's room of a movie theater.

Now, they were in Barry's bedroom and the radio was playing and they were dancing. It was a slow dance and Barry held Matthew in his arms as if he were the girl and pressed against him and whispered instructions in seduction, but as Matthew heard them he heard them as words that Barry might actually have been saying to him.

"You follow the music," he said, "and you look into her eyes, and let your lids get a little heavy and just stay quiet. Follow the music and take her with you. Girls like to follow. So you have to be a strong and confident leader."

Matthew was lost in the rhythm of their movement; it felt real. His cock began to grow in the pouch of his underwear. Barry was not thrown by it.

"That's why it's a good idea to wear a jock. Some girls know what's what, but others can get freaked out and it can get embarrassing."

"I'm sorry," Matthew said.

"Forget it," Barry said. But they had stopped dancing.

Matthew's discomfort was short-lived because it was getting to be the time they were to meet Barry's father. After an early, quick dinner, he was taking them to a night baseball game. Although Matthew had no interest in baseball whatever, that night he worked himself up into a frenzy of excited rooting.

Back at Barry's house, they had ice-cream before they went to bed. Matthew slept in the second twin bed that formed an L with Barry's. In the morning they went to the library where Barry met Brenda and Matthew took the train downtown.

His thoughts swam that weekend and they floated in his mind like bodies resting in the sea facing the open sky. He looked surreptitiously at the male model magazines on the rack without daring to take one down and page through it when he went to the candy store to buy his father a pack of cigarettes.

He hardly could think about how it might have been if Barry, even if only continuing his educational pretense, had kissed him rather than disengaging when he felt Matthew's sexual upsurge.

When Matthew called Barry on Monday night after school, Barry's mother said he was not home. A few days later, he called again.

Barry had not called back. But it was the same thing. Mrs. Hacker was polite. Matthew felt a chill and did not call again. He was not surprised when Barry never called back.

It was probably a good thing that they did not go to the same school. There was no added tension to Matthew's everyday routine, and he could put his momentary embarrassment out of his mind and go on without being reminded too much about his loss.

He was fourteen. He was fifteen. He looked into the windows downtown where the male model magazines were displayed in stores he could not dream of going into. He stared at them. He dreamed of standing like the models, head turned this way and that way, wearing only a posing strap.

He improvised in front of the bathroom mirror before he took a bath. It made him hard and he saw himself in the mirror nearly as if he were a picture to be looked at and not simply an elusive image of himself, the illusory reflection of the person he wanted to be and was not.

He liked the water hot in the bath and sometimes he made it too hot. When he did, he came out dizzy and fell into his swirling bed unable to stand, his head pounding.

"Like what you see?" The voice was friendly. There was no reprimand folded within it. It was not a voice that intended to shame. Nevertheless, Matthew felt ridiculous and embarrassed.

He was waiting for William and had wandered away from the subway kiosk and was looking at the posters of male models posing in the window of the newly installed Hudson's Gym that had opened on Metropolitan Boulevard.

Matthew jumped.

"Hey," Jamie said, "I'm not here to scare you. I want to give you some literature about us. We just opened, and we're inviting everyone in for a free session. It looked from the way you were looking at these pictures," Jamie said pointing, "like you were interested."

Jamie was well built, handsome, and only a few years older. He was wearing tight black short shorts with a thin double red stripe up the sides and a sleeveless black t-shirt with tiny epaulets. It was his work uniform. It made Matthew weak in the knees.

As Matthew was taking one of the brochures, William was coming out of the subway across the street where they had arranged to meet. Matthew saw him and panicked. Without warning, he jumped away, and without being aware of it, he let the papers fall because he suddenly failed to grasp them.

"I gotta go," he said. "There's my friend." He was afraid William had seen them. Jamie picked up the papers.

"Next time," he said, catching Matthew's eyes before he slipped away, looking up at him as he was couching over the papers, "it won't be this easy." He smiled and gave a wink and stood up as Matthew was darting away.

At least, "next time, it won't be this easy" is what Matthew heard, but he could not make sense of it.

"Who was that?" William asked, pointing at Jamie as he entered the gym.

"Some guy giving out coupons for the new gym," Matthew said.

"Just by looking at him you can tell he's worried about the size of his cock," William said.

William was tall and pale and skinny, lanky, and his eyes were piercing, his hair messy, and his voice was raspy and burning with intellect. Without trying he cultivated a circle of listeners around him. He expected to. He was a year ahead of Matthew, a junior when Matthew was a sophomore. Matthew saw him for the first time in the lunch room the second semester when they both had been assigned the same lunch period. He was magnetized by him.

William, who always cultivated a coterie, sensed there was something in Matthew that needed domination, and took him under his wing. New friends excited him, like new-bought books he began to read with eagerness.

Frequently, he embittered the recently prized one after he had read through as much as he wanted to and then stopped, lost interest (was it the book's fault?), shut the book, and put it on the shelf.

"Why do you say that?" Matthew asked.

"Displacement," William said knowingly as they passed through the turnstiles.

"Displacement?" Matthew repeated.

"He's got a cock he's ashamed of because it's little, so he compensates by showing off his muscles. It makes him think he's potent."

"You think so?" Matthew said.

"It's obvious," William said as the doors of the train closed and they were roaring downtown. "All those guys into body building are ashamed of their small penises."

Matthew waited that night until after he finished his geometry homework before he looked at his penis. He didn't think he really cared about its size. Then he remembered the pictures of the guys in the posters in the window of Hudson's. They were awesome, like the guys he couldn't take his eyes off when he looked in the windows downtown at the male models on the covers of the octavo magazines that he never had the courage to purchase.

He had not disputed what William said when he said it. He would not have known what to say had he tried, and William spoke with such finality and authority, with such conviction and certitude, with such a knowing air, that whatever he said seemed incontrovertible. Matthew wanted William to be right. It felt good. It felt like he was being initiated into an understanding of the world he had never had before. Nevertheless, Matthew wondered if it were really true.

Guys went into body building because they were ashamed of their penises? It did not seem to him that the guys posing on the covers of the male model magazines he could not help looking at were ashamed of anything. Nor did that guy Jamie. He wished he looked like them.

Sunday morning he was unable to sleep. He showered and put on jeans and a t-shirt and a pair of moccasins. It was mid-May and overnight it had gotten summery. He took his bike from the storage room in the basement and rode over to the river where the river split into several channels. He chained his bike to one of the girders supporting an overpass and walked along the shore.

The sun was strong and he stripped off his tee-shirt and his jeans and lay down upon the thick grass near the water's edge in just his underwear. He became drowsy and fell asleep. He awoke from the dream that he was taking a shower after gym class and felt an unpredicted rain soaking him.

"How do you like this?" It was someone in a canoe swiftly paddling to the shore and laughing who was calling to him. He stepped out of the canoe in water up to his knees and pulled the canoe onto the shore.

"I didn't expect it was going to rain," Matthew said, as if he had to defend being caught in the rain.

"Neither did I," said the canoeist, laughing as he chained the canoe to a tree.

"You're all wet and so are your clothes," he said as Matthew pulled up his wet jeans and the tee shirt that clung to him.

"I remember you." It was Jamie. "I told you there would be a next time." He was smiling.

"I live nearby. Come over and we can dry off and have coffee."

"My bike is chained up under the bridge."

"Leave it there. It'll be safe. I'll stow my canoe there, too. Come on."

"Ok."

"You don't like being who you are," Jamie said once they'd gotten in out of the rain which had become relentlessly torrential. It was not an accusation; nor was it pity. He was just stating the obvious in a friendly way.

"What's your name?" Matthew said.

"Jamie," the canoeist said. "Why didn't you take the brochure from me? You like those pictures."

Matthew blushed. "I was ashamed to," he said, hoping to get out of it by exculpating himself. But Jamie was not having it.

"Ashamed of what?"

Ashamed of wanting to be like what he liked, of liking it. He did not want to be the way he was and he was not able to be anything but. But he did not say that. He uttered a lame, "I don't know."

"You're ashamed of your body and ashamed of wanting to make it look better. How fucked up is that?"

"Very fucked up," Matthew said. "I guess you're right." He felt an uncanny excitement that he did not trust.

"Did you tell him?" Jamie asked.

"Who?" Matthew said. "What?"

"Your friend whom you ditched me for," Jamie said with a laugh.

"Tell him what?" Matthew said.

"That you are excited by the idea of joining the gym?"

"No."

"You don't talk about that?"

"He thinks it's neurotic."

"What's neurotic?" Jamie said, puzzled. "Joining a gym?"

"Homosexuality."

"Is that the connection you make?"

"Maybe it is," Matthew said.

"So you are excited by the idea of going to the gym, of developing your body, of having a physique you'd be proud to show off and you're ashamed of it because it means you're queer?" Matthew remained silent.

"And it scares you."

Matthew said nothing.

"Because it excites you."

Matthew was feeling dizzy. Jamie was too near him.

"You are afraid of yourself. You are afraid to feel. Like right now, when I'm this close to you, you can't let yourself give in."

Matthew was trembling with the desire to touch him and the inability to do it, but Jamie was not waiting for him. He took hold of his trembling shoulders and looked into his eyes and smiled.

He brought him near and kissed him.

THE END

GIDEON ELLIOT

THE HALF-LIFE OF LOSS

Gay Romance

THE HALF-LIFE OF LOSS

Harold's body was wracked by a fit of coughing and he struggled for breath between coughs. His head ached with fever pain, and his eyes were glassy with illness. He was soaking wet and shivering.

Ben was at his bedside, one hand on his drenched forehead and the other pressed against his back. When Harry was calm enough, he let go of him. He took the pair of dry pajamas and some fresh underwear from on top of the dresser and put them on the table beside the bed.

"Come on, kid. We gotta change you. You're soaked through. Could get sick, you know."

He lifted the quilt and helped Harry sit up. He unbuttoned the tops, pulled the snaps open at the waist and got Harry out of his pajamas. His once well-knit and muscled torso was wasted; his once buff and golden skin torn and blotched and pasty.

"Underwear, too."

He folded him naked inside a big fluffy towel and patted him dry, folded him quickly but meaningfully in his arms, too. Then he helped him into thick socks, underwear, and flannel pajamas. Then he gently toweled his head and combed his hair.

"Now sit in the chair and don't move while I change the bedding," Ben said. "I don't know what I ever saw in you."

Harry was too weak to be irritated. Ben would always be Ben, cheap jokes and all. He sat quietly; he did as he was told. Anyhow, he knew why Ben was doing it and liked him all the more for that. It felt wonderful to be propped against a fluffed up pillow in a dry bed, in dry pajamas, half his face covered by a dry, fresh quilt.

When Lorenzo came home, they brought him a tray with soup and soft, dark bread and then a bowl of steamed organic vegetables and brown rice. He tried, but he could hardly eat any of it. "You guys have really been kind," he scratched out of a broken voice, "but I can't eat it."

Lorenzo kissed him on the forehead. "You're gonna get better. Don't get maudlin."

But he didn't get better. In fact he died.

WHEN BEN and Lorenzo had finally finished with the bureaucracy of death, they collapsed under the weight of grief and spent many days unable to concentrate on anything and broke down crying sometimes alone and sometimes in each other's arms.

Bill Anders at the ad agency told Lorenzo he oughtn't to feel obliged to keep regular hours until he felt he could again. But Lorenzo did not believe in being self-indulgent, found it hard to go against the discipline he prided himself on. So he thanked him and said he would try to follow as much as he could his regular schedule.

Anders came out from behind his desk, took him by the shoulders and looked him in the eyes. Bill Anders knew he had power when he needed it. Now he felt impelled by something in Lorenzo - no, by something in himself regarding Lorenzo.

"This is too important to tough it out," he said. "You do what I tell you." His words had the power he wanted them to have. The tension flashed out of Lorenzo and he collapsed into Anders' arms.

It would be wrong to have sexual feelings at a time like this, gross, exploitative, blasphemous. Nevertheless, Anders did, and he was electrified by a high voltage jolt of desire. It sent a pulse rushing through him. He kissed Lorenzo on the cheek. Lorenzo had already sensed the force of his body, and their magnetic fields directed them. Lorenzo answered his kiss with a more daring kiss until they were tearing at each other with desperate kisses proclaiming by their appropriation of each other that life would not resign its appetite.

They looked at each other afterwards happy with amazement. They had gone deep. They understood each other. It wasn't fair to Ben. They recognized that. They agreed best would be not to mention it. Lorenzo said it and Anders agreed.

Ben sensed something immediately the way a musician knows when a note is going sharp or flat.

"MY BESTFRIEND dies, my lover leaves me, my position at the school is being defunded because of the economy. I'm overwhelmed. And Lorenzo tells me life is a force that insists on living."

"What do you want me to do?"

"Put some quiet in my mind."

"You want me to soothe you?"

"Try to, yes."

"Ben, look at me."

"Yes?"

"Do you think I have no feelings?"

"What are you talking about?"

"What do you think?"

"I don't know. What are you getting at?"

"If I let my tender feelings for you..."

"You're my friend, aren't you?"

"It won't stop there with me. I can't cut myself in two."

"Where are you going with this?"

"Nowhere. I won't do it."

He was unable to say anything, but he knew what she was talking about. He shrugged. "Ok," he said. He left soon after. It was raining. He sat on the cross-town bus. What in the world was he going to do? Everything was equally vacant.

He was diverted for a few minutes by the television. He had heard a little about Todd Bishop. Despite the pugnacious jibes of a right wing ideologue who was trying to undermine him, what he was saying now about getting rid of the anti-marijuana laws made sense. But all that was somewhere else, and here he was where he'd hoped he'd never have to be again -- nowhere!

HE GOT a job as an insurance claims adjuster. It was ironic. He couldn't get over it. Fate was a cynical bitch. He looked at wrecks, then wrote reports describing them and estimated how much they were worth. It was deadly work and he needed the money.

At night he was tired. His brain was turned off and he became incapable of thought. He walked over to Crazy Benny's one Friday night and tried to recharge himself with a brandy.

Chet introduced himself and wondered if he really liked that stuff and Ben confessed he didn't but that his heart had grown cold and one fire to warm it was as good as another and if he didn't like the taste, anyway, he wouldn't miss it when he didn't have it. Chet just looked at him.

"Even if there were no other reason than that to shut you up."

"What?"

But instead of answering he silenced Ben's lips with kisses and pushed his tongue into his mouth as if it were his own domain. Ben stiffened in response and pressed his tongue against Chet's. Chet played with him and then withdrew his mouth. I'll buy you another brandy. It won't burn as much. I promise. He winked.

Ben was face down on the bed, naked, a leather cuff around each wrist and ankle, and from each cuff stretched a chain to one of the four bed posts. A ball-gag in his mouth allowed him to breathe and make sounds, but not to articulate words. Chet was establishing his cock inside him as he teased his back with a short black whip.

Ben threw his head back proudly like a stallion and whinnied. His whole body shook and his bottom started going round at just the same pace as his rider's electric cock pistoning inside him. He bucked and bounded and each time met with his rider's thrust, and each time found himself more firmly ridden, more deeply ploughed. Fingers dug into his nipples, and his master ripped the ball-gag from his mouth and he shrieked as he got fucked, his ass unable to grind his master's cock hard enough.

Chet whipped his muscled shoulders; pressing inside him, drilled his semen into Ben's bowels. "I own you now," he said, growling.

In the morning, Ben did not act as if he'd understood that. So Chet was decidedly cold and explained that Ben would have to go since he was busy the rest of the day. When Ben asked if they might exchange numbers, Chet said, "I don't think so."

Ben froze in the middle of asking if something was wrong. The question was impossible. He was overwhelmed by Chet's absence and his own confusion. He felt like a runner on air between two mountain ledges in a cartoon, who is just looking down and seeing that there is no ground beneath him. He picked his leather jacket up, flung it over his shoulders. "Ciao," he said with what he hoped looked like a friendly smile. "Thanks for the ride."

"Don't mention it."

DEMONS HAD entered his mind and were tormenting consciousness with a death-dance. He couldn't get them to stop. It wasn't only a daytime phenomenon. He had lost the ability to fall asleep.

"Hypnosis," he thought. "Hypnosis." The idea of being hypnotized became an obsession. He brought up the subject whenever he could to see what kind of response he might get. So it wasn't surprising that he was standing beside a wrecked Toyota on an oil stained dirt floor in the back lot of a gas station in Astoria talking to a cute, tough, well-built, blond guy in garage coveralls who'd been inspecting the car -- about hypnosis.

First they talked business. Clay needed the wreck for Urban Melodrama, an installation a group of landscape artists was putting up on a vacant lot off Houston and the Bowery. The car was beyond salvation but it had some scrap value and Ben had to determine what Clay could get it for. As people do when they bargain, they began talking about other things. One thing led to another or at least Ben made it. They went from the driver of the other car's having fallen asleep at the wheel to how the road can hypnotize you, to have you ever been hypnotized? It was a surprise that Clay said he had been and that he'd studied it and had practiced on himself and friends.

"No!" Ben said, up to his ears in interest.

"Yeah," Clay countered. "As an artist," he said, "who wants to hold people's attention with my work, and who wants to get beneath the layers of conscious perception, I find the knowledge of hypnosis is very useful."

"Could you hypnotize me?"

"Do you want to be?" Clay said.

They finished negotiating the car. Clay got off easy. Just had to pay for the towing to lower Manhattan. He invited Ben to come over to his loft the following day, any time after seven. They'd try it.

CLAY HAD the top floor in an old industrial building that had stood vacant for over a decade and then found new life when Soho started to pop. Ben rang the downstairs bell at eight and Clay buzzed him in and was waiting by the elevator, a big open lumbering freight cage of wire mesh. He was wearing leather pants and no shirt. Ben felt weak looking at him.

Clay led him through a twisting passage to a steel door. Beyond that a small vestibule opened into a grand space made of several large rooms to the left and then a great open room with windows on three sides that looked out over the city. They smoked a joint and looked at the New York night skyline.

"Get comfortable," Clay said. "Sit in this chair, and look at me. Watch the pendant I'm holding. There. Do you see it begin to swing? Follow the swing of the pendant as if your eye-strings were tied to it."

AS BEN'S eyes grew heavy, the focus of their attention shifted from the swinging pendulum to the inescapable depths of Clay's eyes. Their power overwhelmed him. He felt a large space being carved out inside him. Inside that hollow he felt a craving need for Clay. He wanted to worship him.

He heard the sound of water rushing, and saw the shimmering surface of a rushing brook. He felt its frosty waters washing over his naked body until he was transformed. Something he did not like about himself, some filthy appendage that was not him but had come to define and characterize him had been scrubbed away. He was lying bronzed in the blazing sun on a ledge of red rock on the edge of a broad-backed lake. He felt the bundles of his muscles stretch to their fullest and a sleek garment of tight flesh cover them. Where his mind had been now there was only a golden radiance and an inescapably beautiful music that was always just beyond hearing.

When he woke up Clay was straddling him and he was looking into the tunnel of his eyes. Clay took hold of his stiff cock and pressed it to his own. He did not resist. Clay lowered his head and kissed him on the mouth, sucking his breath out of him and giving his own back to him.

Ben did not want to see Lorenzo but Lorenzo spotted him on Mercer Street before he could turn the corner. "What have you done to yourself?" Lorenzo asked almost in awe.

"What do you mean?"

"You look terrific."

"Thanks," Ben said with scorn.

"Hey, don't be mad."

"I gotta run."

"Don't you have time for a coffee? I never see you anymore."

"I gotta run," Ben said, and left Lorenzo standing there watching with lust as he walked swiftly away from him. He wandered without direction for a while with a troubled mind, unable to stop it from whirring, and unable to hold on to any thought. He felt a crack, a fissure running through him, and through that crack, he felt his spirit leaking away. He punched Clay's number on his cell and Clay picked up.

"Hey, I'm not sure why I called. I was just..."

"Come over."

"I don't want to bother you."

"Come over now. Where are you?"

"On Wooster Street, near where the old firehouse used to be."

"You're not far. Come over." He hung up.

CLAY HAD a cup of green tea waiting and told Ben to drink it, and then said very quietly, "I am here," and Ben lowered the cup onto its saucer. He looked into Clay's eyes and said "Thank you," and then, quite beyond himself, he began to cry. It embarrassed him, and he could not stop it. Clay took him in his arms and consoled him. Consolation turned to love making. He drew his fingers over Ben's lips and made him smile through his tears.

"Breathe," he said, and gently rubbed his nipples.

BEN WAS filled with the desire to please Clay, and he wanted Clay to be proud of him and to be worthy of Clay's admiration. He stopped assessing wrecks. He gave up his room in Park Slope. He moved into the loft. He became Clay's secretary, assistant, cook, body servant, publicist, and slut. He wore black eye-liner and short black leather shorts with side slits, and boots up to his knees. He shaved his chest and wore a black leather collar and a triple-banded silver ring on his left middle finger. He found a chromium cock ring while going through Clay's jewelry box once and asked if he might wear it.

Clay smiled and nodded. "Take your shorts off," he said, and the briefs. Ben stood before him erect.

"It won't work if you're erect," he laughed, and gently began to rub Ben's cock until a frenzy of energy rippled through him and he came.

Clay eased one testicle from inside Ben's scrotum through the circle of the cock ring and then helped the one behind it through too. "No hard-on," he said, and licked Ben's cock so it was slippery enough to worm through into the circle. He had to be quick because it was beginning to stiffen again, anyhow. Once the ring was secured at its base, a tight cap around cock and balls, the cock stood hard as steel and sharp as a blade.

Clay pushed him onto the bed so that he lay on his back, then cuffed his hands together behind his head. Beginning at his arm pits he scratched his nails across Ben's chest, teasing his nipples with increasing pain, but it kept dissolving into ecstasy. He took the stiff and starving cock into his mouth and tongued its slot and took it all the way to the back of his throat. It felt like he had enclosed it in the depths of himself and he kept sucking it with his throat as his tongue stroked it.

CLAY NEVER did that again, and Ben never forgot it and always longed for it, hoped for it, held himself back from begging for it for fear of displeasing Clay. But Ben did a lot of cock sucking himself after that. Clay liked to pick a stud up on the street and film Ben sucking him. Getting Sucked premiered at a loft on Prince Street. J. Hoberman from The Voice jumped up and down about it and then Richard Brody wrote a defense of it in The New Yorker, and then A.O. Scott turned it into a gold mine in The Sunday Times, where Manohla Dargis, a week later, said it was the first thing she'd seen since Jack Smith's Flaming Creatures that had anything to contribute to the archeology of sexual desire.

THE END

GIDEON ELLIOT

THEN THERE WERE NONE

Gay Romance

THEN THERE WERE NONE

Why, let the stricken deer go weep,
The hart ungalled play,
For some must watch, while some must sleep.
Thus runs the world away.

~*Hamlet*~

It had been a long time since I had felt anything like a spark of sexual excitement pulsing through me and strengthening my body or charging my spirit. My mind was crowded with a merry-go-round of useless memories. The same scenes, the same unanchored thoughts, over and over, revolved and revolved inside my head.

One night, as it was my habit, my compulsion, as I cruised the streets of Lower Manhattan, with heaviness in my limbs, it was as if something had changed, somewhere far away, that would affect me where I was and determine where I would go. Its reverberation, its shock wave traveled a great distance and engulfed me. Out of the corner of my eye, I noticed somebody passing.

Idly, ritually, without expectation, I looked over my shoulder. It was one time too many doing what I had too often hopelessly, fruitlessly done. I saw something. There was someone who mesmerized me, who met my gaze, caught it and kept it. I was turned around, and I walked back to from where I had just come even though I was weary and wanted to go home, disillusioned to the point of weariness, having had enough of not having enough, wary about picking guys up on the street. I answered his smile with a defeated smile of my own and a shake of the head.

"I'm weary and I'm on my way home. At least that's where I was headed before I turned around and saw you." I added that when I saw his smile deepen; our eyes met.

"It's going to rain," he said. "Come up to my place. We can smoke a joint, I'll put some music on, and maybe we can sleep together tonight. Tomorrow's Saturday. Do you have to be somewhere in the morning?"

He spoke without the slightest hesitation or doubt so openly about things that ought to have been so distant between strangers, defiantly but affectlessly asserting an intimacy between us that came into being only because he acted like it was already there.

"No," I said. "No, I don't." He did not know, I thought, how much there was no place I had to be tomorrow or any morning.

He put his arm around me and pressed me to him. He was strong and muscular and I felt myself yielding to him. His body was hard and tight, like mine had been. His eyes were soft and penetrating. "Let's go," I said.

"It isn't far," he said.

He lived by the Hudson, on the top floor of a reconditioned loft, just south of Fourteenth Street. It had once been a warehouse. You could see the river and across it to the new outlined skyline of New Jersey.

"My father spent his life hauling sides of beef down there," he said as we stood by the window where the crowds of overdressed office workers by day spent their nights pretending they were celebrities, fashion models in magazines or stars in the movies with wild hair and slicked-down hair and spiked heels and manicured moustaches.

"Everybody in Rutherford – that's where my family is from, Rutherford, New Jersey" – told him he was crazy when he bought this building and the one next door for ten thousand dollars in 1974, but he laughed and ignored them, and "I sold the other building for almost twenty-three million dollars last fall, and I kept this one, renovated the whole thing, made a penthouse for myself and rent out the middle floors residentially and the ground floor commercially."

He rolled a joint as he spoke, and we smoked and then he put on some Billie Holliday and, as corny as it may seem, when he took me in his arms, we danced, and then he kissed me and very gently started stroking me.

"I want to fuck you," he whispered. "I want you to fuck me," I answered. "I'm going control of you," he said. "I want to surrender to you," I said. "You have no other choice," he said. "I know," I said.

On my knees, bowed low before him, very slowly and with great devotion I took his ankle in my palms, put my lips to his instep and began pouring myself out to him. I tongued his foot and became hard like iron. A feeling of worshipfulness, of gratitude flooded through me, gratitude that he was there and allowing me to worship him.

He lifted me and kissed me and ran his fingers across my nipples and led me to his bed and undressed me and stood me at the foot of his bed and gazed at me and appraised me as he stripped his shirt off and took off his trousers. He was like iron, like a magnet. I quivered involuntarily and felt myself lurch towards him. He guided me backwards supine upon the bed. He spread my legs and raised them and gazed into my eyes and kissed me and told me I belonged to him and slowly back and forth dug himself deeper into me as I gasped and called him master and I surrendered to him.

Afterwards we sat leaning on the pillows propped against the headboard, caressing each other. Outside rain was falling.

"I worship you," I said.

He nodded. "I know," he said. "You aren't the first."

"And I know I won't be the last," I said. "But it doesn't change it."

"No," he said.

We woke up late, nearly noon, roused by the telephone. It had begun to snow. He spoke briefly. I did not listen but found the coffee and made two cups of espresso. He smiled a thank you as he took hold of the coffee by the saucer, and the phone rang again. I dressed as he spoke, hoping we might walk by the river, but he told me I had to go home.

I asked him when we might see each other again. I was not inexperienced. I knew the things that were said at night usually lost their power in the morning. A man who had been closest to you, who had finally arrived after you had waited so long, and almost given up hope, could drop you out of his life as if you had never touched, even after he had penetrated so deeply into you that he'd gone to the places in you that you knew were there but you had only been able to imagine and never had been able to get to yourself.

He kissed me and as I parted my lips after his kiss to speak, he put his finger over them, forbidding me, and I understood I had to leave. I bowed my head to him and kissed his hand. He smiled a parting smile to me. I opened the elevator door and went in. My heart was flying high as the elevator dropped. I realized soon my heart would too. I started to remember something. And then I forgot.

He did drop out of my life as if we had never touched. There apparently was no other way. But he left the thought of himself with me and although he was not present, he was always present, or, better, he was always an absent presence.

Many times, I looked for him on the street, and I often walked passed his loft, but something prevented me from ringing his bell. I felt like I needed his permission to do that. I did not feel like I had it. So I prevented myself.

Once I saw him walking by the river with his arm around a boy, but there was nothing I could do. I gazed at the water.

When Mickey Gallant broke down after Buzz left him, I was calmer than I ever would have been in the past. It was several months later.

I had been in love with Mickey for nearly five years. It had been torment. It had been stupid. It had been out of my control. I knew it had been crazy. There was nothing to bring us together or to hold us together, no common interests and activities -- except I was overawed by him and wanted to melt into him. He was a jock, watched a lot of television, worked, as an accountant, in an upscale haberdashery. He was graceful and gorgeous and gallant like his name, and his eyes said I love you to everything they saw.

At first I ached for him and then my desire turned into a caustic bitterness. I had contempt for the way he was and the way he lived. But it didn't help. I continued to ache for him.

That he just was not attracted to me made me feel inferior to him. It had not make sense, it was not fair that he did not desire me, that his soul was not swooning for me. I would not let myself believe it. His eyes always said something else no matter what he said.

I often had felt foolish and inadequate with him. Had I looked at it objectively, there was no reason he should care for me. I had become stupid. I would be sullen or petulant or snide and sarcastic. Often I had made him lose patience and become cold.

He called me on a Tuesday night after eleven, and asked me to meet him. He was in a broken state. It was astonishing to see. He had not shaved. We sat in the Lion's Head and got drunk. I listened to him as he chain smoked Gauloise and told me about how much he had not realized how much Buzz meant to him. Then without warning, he was talking about his father's death, suicide in Montana. And his mother's re-marriage. He began to cry. I took his hand and held it tenderly and realized this was a fantasy come true. But I felt nothing.

When Buzz returned after a confusing week of telephone calls and anger that the two of them endured, I was glad for them both, that they had gotten through it.

"You know I hesitated to call you," Mickey said, as we three sat in their living room smoking a joint and drinking coffee. "But I gambled on the fact that in the end I could rely on you. Thanks."

"I'm sorry I have been such an ass-hole," I said.

"When you hurt, you hurt," he said. "I can't change my feelings. But that's not your fault."

For the first time he had acknowledged me.

"It's not yours either," I responded in a voice that almost had no sound.

"But I know what it is like," he said.

Months passed. April came. The ginkgo trees were in bud. It had been raining all day, but when I went out cruising that night, it was not raining anymore. But, the air smelled of rain. The newly emerging leaves smelled of rain. My heart was full of rain. I walked slowly through the winding streets of Greenwich Village like a person in a fever, a gentle fever that released me from all the responsibilities of being in the everyday world. I began to rain.

The green and red extended lines of street light reflections in the still-wet blacktop where few cars rolled struck me to the heart.

"As you read this, you are becoming aware that an old and familiar feeling of submission is overwhelming you and is pulling you deeper into a state of total surrender. It is a frightening experience and it makes you tremble. Trembling itself takes you deeper and deeper down into the bottomless pit of self-abasement until you feel yourself entirely emptied out of all identity and you feel yourself going deeper and deeper into pure slavedom."

My eyes closed. I kept circling back and reading the same words again and again on the Hypno/Trance website until I shut the lid of my laptop and got into my bed, where I lay the way I fell, unable to move.

In the morning when I checked my e-mail as I routinely do every morning, that compelling message was there, now, automatically sent to me from the site I had visited. I opened it and read it again.

"As you read this you are becoming aware that an old and familiar feeling of submission is overwhelming you and is pulling you deeper into a state of total surrender. It is a frightening experience and it makes you tremble. Trembling itself takes you deeper and deeper down into the bottomless pit of self-abasement until you feel yourself entirely emptied out of all identity and you feel yourself going deeper and deeper into pure slavedom."

Once again I started reading the words over and over, and once again I became unbearably sleepy until my head dropped into the cradle of my arms spread across my desk in front of my open computer.

THE END

GIDEON ELLIOT

Repetitions
GAY ROMANCE

<u>REPETITIONS</u>

Banish, first,
dreams that enslave us:
silver of stars,
night's desire;
evening's fire,
The envy of morning.

The Earth Turns

How often now they return to me, those nights I stood under the trestle waiting for him. At first, I still expected him to come. Later, I knew he wouldn't. But there I was, posed against one of the supporting pillars, waiting for him.

The nights were brown. The streets were woozy with tiredness. I pushed through waves of unbreathable air. Where the trucks used to park, someone wanted to piss on me. Smiling, I declined and kept walking.

I saw him in the distance: leaning against the fluorescent theater window display, on the other side of Hudson Street; someone was there, not the one I'd been waiting for, my heart's master who had abandoned me, but another one. I breathed deeply, relaxing and becoming tense in the same moment. I slowed my walk down and became very smooth. A smile crept onto my face. It sat easily on my lips. As I approached him, it broke into a grin. I caught him.

"Hi," he said, responding to my as-yet-silent greeting.

"Hello," I said.

"You going home?" he said.

"You want to come with me?"

We were both cool. We knew what we wanted. There was no
need to go through preliminaries. The best talking is done in silence. We
took each other's hand and sauntered as we walked, each, making the
other float with the joy of feeling the world starting over again. I let us in
and I looked at him. He was even better in the light.

"I'll get a candle and shut that," I said, as I took one out of a box
of utility candles I kept in the freezer. I swiveled it into the empty
candlestick on the table. I struck the match and shut the overhead light at
the same time and then I put the match to the wick. There was a small
ball of flame giving a dim light until the fire shot up the wick in a fluted
oval and gave the room dark amber yellow candle-light. I shook the
match out just as I began to feel the burn of the flame on my fingertips.

He grasped my balls with his hand and drew my mouth to his
and pulled me entirely into him. I wrapped my left arm about him and
held his neck in my palm and breathed my whole life into him and felt
him breathe it back to me inside his own. I tasted the pot on his tongue.

"You got more smoke?" I said.

"Sure," he answered and dug a slightly smoked joint out of his
jeans, lit it by flipping a zippo, took a deep drag and then pressed his lips
to mine and blew a heavy blast of smoke through my lungs and into my
belly. My shaved chest heaved as if it would explode but it swelled into
an imploring kiss grinding me more deeply into him, swooning with the
pleasure of his body.

He told me he wanted to hypnotize me, that he wanted to have
me completely in his power. He said this as he held me in his arms, and
after every word he kissed my lips. My head was spinning with desire for
him. All I could think was how much I belonged with him.

He put his hand on my cock repeating that he wanted to make
me his slave, to dominate me, and command me, and have me obey him.

He kissed me between each word. His words fell slowly on me like the rain in spring when you're young. My lips were quivering with kisses for him.

I became his slave. I repeated the spell he whispered. I was in his power. I heard him say, "You are mine tonight." I heard him say that I was in a trance that I had surrendered my will to him and become his slave. I had no wish to resist him. I liked this game, but I panicked the next moment. I had stepped into something I could not step out of. It was not going to end in the morning. Everything was up to him. I could only hope he would be kind to me.

His finger up my ass at that very moment was right. I let out a long breath and threw my head all the way back. He took me by the chin and pushed his index finger into my mouth and down my throat. He had me at both ends. I was his. I sucked on him through both my holes. He brought his head down to the level of my chest, tilted it slightly and bit my nipple. My body writhed. My cock throbbed. His fist was wrapped fast around it blocking release.

Pulling his hand from my mouth, he slapped my face hard, not loosening his grip on my cock. I felt the sting and the wetness of my own saliva. It felt good to belong to someone again.

Life Goes On

I saw him looking at me. I watched him walk over. I accepted his cigarette. He lit it for me, cupping the match in his palms. I inhaled deeply and blew out the smoke with a relaxation I hadn't felt for days.

"Coffee?" he said.

"Sure," I said.

One thing was as good as another. I could spend an hour with him. Even more. And if he wanted to fuck, it was ok with me. I'm good at it. I do it several times a week with a bunch of different guys. Some are surprised, they say, that someone who -- here they falter – you know, looks like you [me], I mean, you're, you know, in a category beyond good looking, that someone who looks like me would be interested in ordinary looking guys who don't carve their bodies with daily workouts, the way I do. "Why not?" I reply. "You can tell a slave by his physique. Not a Master." I smile. I can tell by their eyes how deeply they want me.

Anyhow we sat in Smiler's for coffee, and I saw that he was nervous.

"Why you nervous?" I said.

"My, we are direct."

I ignored his camp. "You're nervous," I said. "Why?"

He stared at his hands. How could he tell me? He wasn't nervous. He was trembling with desire for me. It was so strong, his desire for me, that it made his bones rattle and his body shake. He couldn't keep his teeth from chattering, hard as he tried, and clamped down on his jaw.

"Tell me," I commanded.

He looked at my face to see how he ought to take those words and saw that I was impenetrably serious, and it worked on him like a medicine, and he became calm.

"I want to kiss your feet."

Things Burn

Crazy Benny's was boarded up after the fire. Flowers, teddy bears, Judy Garland CDs, black leather harnesses and other such items were placed outside in a large crate in memory of Rory, one of the bartenders. Police and fire officials had no doubt that it was arson and promised swift action.

Benny announced at a neighborhood meeting that he would reopen. Right there people began pledging contributions earmarked for rebuilding. A steering committee was formed and three months later, after mentions in The Times, The Voice, The New Yorker, and on several radio stations, an amazing $643,281.67 had been donated.

I had gone out on the fire escape to get a little air. It was a large loft, and it was packed – hundreds of guys, each more of a killer than the next. Who was the hottest depended on who you were looking at. I was dizzy. It was a still July night, quite warm, and it was only the proximity of New York Bay that gave the air a current slighter than a breeze but nevertheless noticeable.

I felt a hand pressing against my bare chest and the fingers gently twisting my nipple. I started to turn my head to see who it was when I felt his warm breath on my neck and I shivered.

"Don't move," he said. "You are mine tonight."

A Mobius Strip

They come, they go, they come back again. They leave again -- old ones, new ones, hopeful ones. But here I am. Here I remain.

The river flows; I stay still. It makes sense. I like it when they parade by and stop now and then for climactic moments.

But I don't stay with them. A side effect? Literature becomes necessary. So I write these stories conjuring up possibilities, amazing phantoms I want to transmute into flesh, whose kisses you feel when you breathe.

After the Kiss

It was a leaden day in August. It had been raining since last night. Bank Street crossed Fourth five stories below. Dawn was just spreading like gun metal through the layers of the sky.

He yawned. I held his face.

"You are beautiful," I said.

"You are very promiscuous, aren't you?"

I grinned.

"Don't be coy," he said. "It's ok. It's gonna make it even better when you can't get hard for anyone but me."

Lost Moments

I saw her walking out of a café with Erick at her side. I tottered, but I kept my balance even if not my inner composure. I remembered how I had given her up, thrown her away. I remembered how he had once pressed himself against me and taken me with a kiss when he was drunk. The loss was tragic, but somehow – I still wasn't sure how – essential. I remembered her bitter coldness and the toneless, bitten down curse she uttered when I left. I shook then. I was shaken. She might have let me go cleanly without trying to wound, leaving a bruise.

Our paths crossed. She recognized me and smiled with a hint of triumphant irony. I nodded my head and smiled acknowledging hers. We passed on without stopping. She hadn't gotten older. She was only more beautiful. Erick was somewhere else.

I walked over to McDougal Street and headed for The Peacock, pocketed in the winding alley that connects McDougal and Sixth Avenue.

It was dark and woody inside, and nobody bothered you if you…if it wasn't tobacco in your pipe. I ordered a small café a la française, put enough sugar in to make it sweet and took a few pulls on my pipe and then tamped it.

Jenny was on tonight and had brought over the espresso.

She was a beauty, and sweet with a gentle kindness and a melancholy listlessness. She was lithe, soft, and angular. She had thick curly brown hair like a poodle. Her features were sharp. Her mouth was full and rich and her white teeth sparkled, but not as incandescently as her eyes.

"Hello, Jenny," I said.

"I'm so glad to see you," she said as if repeating a lesson.

"Tell me why," I said.

"Because I need to see you."

"Why do you need to see me?"

"Because without you I am nothing."

It was quiet and it was late and Jenny had no trouble getting Marie to let her leave work early.

We headed over to her place on Fourth Street off the Bowery.

She was warm when she was naked. She was ripe with a richness that was overwhelming and a juiciness that made you want just to gush her up. She looked at me with big, happy eyes and we kissed like we were singing songs.

She was quiet in the morning. Hanging her head down, but looking up over her defeat with gentle but gone eyes, she said, "We shouldn't see each other again."

I understood her. My eyes went too. They were happy but gone, and I understood her.

A Parting Glance

I looked at him from a distance. I had never seen the ideal male form so perfectly embodied. I couldn't take my eyes away and stood transfixed on the corner watching.

An orange shirt with tiny sleeves clung to his torso and stopped before his ribbed midriff. He wore a pair of tight fitting short brown corduroy shorts, slit at each side and a pair of Roman sandals with leather cords that laced up to his knees forming a diamond pattern up his calves. His beautiful handsome face had no trace of disdain in it.

Another guy, just about as good as him, wearing tight jeans and a burgundy chest-hugging polo shirt met him. They took each other by the shoulders. Quick on the lips they kissed. Then hand in hand they were soon out of sight.

THE END

GIDEON ELLIOT

ENTIRELY JASON

GAY ROMANCE

ENTIRELY JASON

Elliott crushed out another cigarette. He finished his buttered muffin with a swallow of cold coffee, fished in his pocket for three crumpled dollar bills, and left them, balled up from his damp fist, upon the table top. He slid out of the booth, slung his green book bag over his shoulder and rushed out of the luncheonette onto a crowded Broadway.

He was wheezing as he took the steps at Philosophy Hall and damp with perspiration, he sat slouching in his chair in the lecture hall. Professor Dupee was explaining the significance of Forster's idea of "connecting" and what his debt was to Shelley's great ode on the death of Keats. "'The one remains,'" he quoted, dragging on a cigarette. "Mrs. Wilcox has been," he continued, "transmuted from a person into the central idea of the novel, becoming its unifying spirit."

Elliott cut gym and stayed reading in Butler library until after night had fallen, then walked back to his room on a hundred and sixth street after ten. His eyes were aching.

Not just in song, but in fact, autumn in New York is a difficult time for people who are alone. In Elliott's case, an inchoate longing without an object plagued him like a physical symptom of an undiscoverable disease.

Fagged out from jerking off without coming and unable to sleep, he got dressed and walked south along Central Park West down to Columbus Circle and then back. The air was balmy. He didn't walk on the park side. There, statuesque guys in tight jeans and body hugging muscle shirts slouched against the low stone wall. Some lounged on the benches lining the street. Others were poised with cigarettes and distant countenances, advertisements for themselves. He kept to the west side of the street, passing the façades of the sumptuous towers where wealth and glamour had installed their favorites.

Friday night he went over to the Student Activities Cinema Festival at McMillin for a screening of Zazie, and Malle was there afterwards taking questions.

He smoked several cigarettes in the lobby, furtively envied several couples, got a headache from the film, didn't stay around for Louis Malle and wandered downtown along Broadway afterwards. At the seventy-second street kiosk a drunk called out to him, "Hey pretty boy, wanna suck my dick? He turned away from the man's glance with a show of angry disgust.

HE DIDN'T look good. He had let himself put on weight, was ill-groomed, unkempt, and thoughtlessly attired, and he knew it. He was depressed. In recovery, he said, but not recovered. It had been over a year however since he'd been dumped. It haunted him that the reason Ellen had left him was because he hadn't made her feel that he wanted her enough. He had not made her feel "like she was a woman," she said. But, it was strange, he only felt -- really, painfully felt - that he wanted her at those times when she withdrew from him. Then he would always become terrifically attentive, even charming, and she'd bounce back. But it couldn't last.

Sometimes, when he was stoned, he could con himself into seeing himself in a better light. He kept trying to improve, but hardly succeeded. So he tried to ignore all that and assert himself intellectually wherever he could. The result was that he seemed opinionated and little aware of the feelings of others or how to behave properly. And nobody listened to him anyhow.

He tried to inure himself. "Cast a cold eye," he repeated sotto voce.

BUT IT didn't work. His eyes were anything but cold. They were hot with desire, burning with hopeless longing; simultaneously he looked and pulled his glance away. He failed in everything he approached, and he could not approach anything he wanted. The astonishing times he succeeded, it had no permanence; it wasn't part of something firmly anchored that was continually building.

It all showed in the way he took those walks along Central Park West so many nights. What was it but unadmitted cruising? And he knew it, although he denied it.

Words spun through his head. Thoughts rushed around, transformed into other thoughts and dissolved, like clouds. He was anchored by a tension created by the collision of desire and denial. Both dominated him, and he performed -- as if awake and conscious -- within the deep trance created by their interlock. Aimless, he passed wasted time; life evaporated.

His fantasy, of course, was that this would change. But he was not able to change it -- just as when he cruised he could not approach cruising. He longed for cruising to approach him; for something besides negation to approach and change him.

ELLIOTT WAS walking back up Central Park West, across the street from the park. A good looking, well-built, sandy-haired guy who had been browsing a few nights ago at the New Yorker Bookstore -- he'd noticed him there - was walking behind him, then passed him, but waited for the light at the corner. It was 81st Street. They had just passed the Natural History museum. The Planetarium was down the block if you went left.

"You were at the New Yorker Bookstore the other night."

"I saw you there."

"Do you live around here?"

"On a hundred and sixth street. You?"

"Ninety sixth."

"I go to Columbia."

"So do I. What do you study?"

"Physics and psychology."

"Good god!"

"You?"

"Comp. Lit., Art History," Elliott said.

"I live on this block. You want to come up?"

"Sure."

It was a one bedroom on the top floor of a brownstone. Marshall's heart was beating with anxiety when they reached the fifth floor, and Elliott was trying to suppress his huffing.

The key turns in the lock. The door opens.

"Come in," Marshall said and he flicked on the light. "You want anything to drink?"

"No. No thanks; nothing."

"Do you smoke," he asked meaningfully. "I mean..."

"You mean... do you have?"

"A bit of the weed."

Marshall took a small silver tin from the utensils drawer built into the apron of the kitchen table. They were sitting across from each other at the table. They got stoned together and soon by some unrecorded movement of agreement began looking at each other and staring into each other's eyes. Seated though they remained they felt each the sensation of rising energy that pulled up from the weight of their bodies.

"Want to try something?" Marshall asked.

"What?"

"Have you ever been hypnotized."

"Can you?"

"Would you like to be?"

"I'll try it."

"Does it frighten you?"

"It excites me."

"What about it excites you?"

Elliott hesitated.

"If we're going to do this you have to be honest."

"Surrendering," Elliott blurted out.

"How would you feel about obeying me?"

Elliott was silent.

"No hesitation. You have to say the truth."

"The idea excites me...and it frightens me."

Marshall held a crystal pendant in front of Elliott and guided him.

"Look at the pendant and follow it as I swing it back and forth. Good. I want you to forget your name. When you open your eyes, you won't remember your name. But when I tell you what your name is, you will know that it is your name, and you will know that because I name you I possess you. Do you understand?"

"I belong to you."

"Very good. Now open your eyes."

Elliott opened his eyes, squinted and shook his head, momentarily disoriented, until he recalled where he was.

"Hey, I'm sorry," he said. "I must've zoned out."

"It's getting late," Marshall said as if in response. "Maybe you ought to be going home."

"Guess so," Elliott said, disappointed, but unsure why.

"You want to get together again?" Marshall asked.

"Sure," Elliott said.

Pushing a message pad and ball point pen towards him Marshall said, "Here, write down your name and phone number."

Elliott scribbled his phone number first. It came to him immediately, but when he started to write his name, he hesitated. He looked up puzzled. He couldn't remember it.

"Is something the matter?" Marshall asked.

"No. I mean, this is absurd, but I can't... remember my name."

"You can't remember your name?"

"I can't."

"Try."

"I am."

"Well?"

"Nothing."

"You alright?"

"I think so."

"Well, what about other things? Where do you live?"

"One fifteen a hundred and sixth street," Elliott said without missing a beat.

"Where do you go to school?"

"Columbia."

"What year are you in?"

"Senior."

"How old are you?"

"Twenty-two."

"What's your name?"

Blank.

"You remember everything else."

"I can't remember my name."

"Shall I tell it to you?"

"Please."

"It's Jason."

"Jason, of course!" Elliott said smiling with relief.

"Can you remember it now?"

"It's Jason."

Marshall snapped his fingers. "Just like that," he said, the words he had instructed Elliott would trigger his trance.

Immediately Elliott - now Jason - fell back into a trance.

"Can you hear me, Jason?"

"Yes, sir."

"I am pleased with you."

"Thank you, sir."

"Jason, I am going to re-shape you. You will lose your old identity. Elliott will disappear. You will be what I make of you."

"Yes, sir."

FROM THE start, Elliott felt different. After three months, he actually was different, physically, emotionally, sexually. He carried himself more easily, was calmer, less anxious, more focused and more able to concentrate than previously. He began swimming daily and used the weight room, too. He became unable to stomach coffee and loathed cigarettes. His taste for food changed. Bagels and muffins and sodas and hamburgers became noxious to him. He became fastidious with regard to his clothing. He could not bear even to touch most of what he used to wear. He became interested in sketching and began painting. He was good.

The arrogant cringing was gone. So too was the clammy, doughy-textured
skin and the sense of avoidance or withdrawal. He became open-shouldered, graceful, inviting and engaging, trim muscled and well-defined, friendly with his body. It was an astounding change to everyone who had known him, to everyone except himself. As far as he knew, he had always been this way.

MARSHALL'S HAND was covering his and their heads were close. The table cloth was burgundy, and the meal was nearly finished. They were sharing a joint. Chamber music by Faure was playing on NCN. The candles were low.

"I saw you a few times around Columbia before we met, even before the time at the New Yorker Bookstore. You fascinated me because I knew you were getting in the way of the person you really are. I wanted to know him, I found him very attractive. But he wasn't there. You were keeping him prisoner, had him locked up. He couldn't get out.

"So I took a strong dislike to you, stronger as I became more strongly attracted to him because you were keeping me from him by keeping him from me. Sometimes I felt like beating the shit outta you, and it's lucky for you that I'm a pacifist." He smiled, and continued. "I knew what he was like even before he was entirely there. And I knew I had to get to him...which getting hostile with you would never accomplish."

Elliott had become Jason almost entirely by now. He sat quietly, a calm glow on his face looking intently at Marshall and listening to him with real attention.

"I understand why I feel such devotion to you," he said.

"Thank you," Marshall said. "I had to get you away from yourself in order to have you."

"By doing that you've made me myself, too. It's weird. I really wasn't who I was until now."

It wasn't complete however. Jason had a native intelligence, a vital narcissism, a healthy exhibitionism and a generous disposition, but he hadn't declared his homosexuality. He hadn't gotten to the bottom of himself acknowledging, celebrating the reality that he was most himself and most in possession of himself when he surrendered himself sexually and could be devoted to a man through whom and for whom he existed.

Marshall snapped his fingers. "Just like that," he said. "Stand up, Jason," he said. "Let me admire my work. I did good work." He put his hands on Jason's waist, drew him near, and kissed him on the lips. Jason shivered.

"Did you know you were gay?"

"I was afraid of it," Jason said. "When I walked at night on Central Park West I was tormented with desire and dread, and I felt dull and stale."

THE FIRST warm sun of April was breaking through the winter sky. Elliott was nowhere to be seen. Jason's hair, dyed a sandy blond now, was perfectly trimmed and deliberately shaggy. He had on a worn dungaree jacket hanging open over a midnight blue turtle neck, faded jeans and snug high boots underneath them. Bus driver sunglasses covered his eyes. He wore a gold watch with a leather bracelet on his left wrist and a jade stone set in a silver ring on his right pinkie.

Marshall was standing by the fountain near the arch.

"Now I have to wait for you," he said as if observing an irony.

"Forgive me, Master," Jason said before kissing him on the lips and lingering with his tongue. "I got it."

"Good boy. I knew it. I'm proud of you."

"You should be proud of yourself," Jason laughed. "Whatever I accomplish, it's only because of you."

"That's not entirely true."

"You knew it was there. But it was only there because you knew that and could bring it out in me."

"I knew you were there, and I knew I had to have you."

"You got me."

"And I'm keeping you."

THE END

Here is a sample from another story you may enjoy:

GIDEON ELLIOT
Sweet
SURRENDER
Gay Compilation 4
GAY BONDAGE EROTICA

THEY MET on St. Mark's Place outside The Taberna, a Greek place that Mark knew. It had begun to snow. They both arrived in front of the restaurant at the same time and embraced. No one had to wait outside in the cold for the other, stamping his feet.

"It's good to see you. I'm really sorry about last night," Mark said, a lovely smile gracing his face. But Tayler was not having it and told him he had nothing to apologize for although he might have a lot to think about.

"Like what?" Mark asked without rancor.

Tayler drew in his breath. "Like what you keep avoiding."

"What's that?"

"I don't know," Tayler said. "It just seems to me you are trying to blank something out."

You're so analytical," Mark said gently taking Tayler's cheeks in his palm and drawing his lips to him.

"Not here," Tayler said.

"And why not here?" Mark said.

"Look at your menu."

"Octopus."

"Octopus?"

"I like it," Mark said. "And vine leaves. They're good here."

So they both had a vinegar drenched grilled octopus and stuffed vine leaves and Tayler liked them. But he was easy to please, anyhow.

"Will you go with me next Friday night?" Mark said.

"You know what you're doing?"

"Yeah, being who I am. Openly, as they say."

Tayler shrugged. Outside, the snow had begun to fall again.

"Why else you want me to go?"

"Because I'm starting to feel like I need to be with you all the time. I'm complete only when I'm with you. Otherwise I'm missing something. Do you feel that way about me?"

"Do you think I'd surrender that kind of information to a sadist like you?"

"Torture will open your lips."

"So will kisses," Tayler said coming closer.

"In that case," Mark said, but the rest of his words were smothered in a kiss.

THEY WERE like two Greek warriors horsing around, wrestling with each other on the plains of Troy. Naked, their bodies glinted bronze in the evening light. They looked as if they were still clad in breastplates. As the blazing sun inched its orange-saturated ball downwards, it fell behind the distant jagged mountains. Then it became impossible to distinguish between rock and the ether.

They strained their muscles in the simultaneous effort to seize and to evade until the force of the power that strove through them brought their lips together and the kiss only intensified their struggle.

Tayler gave an open-throated yawn and squeezed Mark's hand as they walked through the chill air of Manhattan in December.

"I love you," Mark said.

"It's mutual," Tayler said. He meant it, but he was pessimistic. The surface often has a way of disappearing leaving you stuck somewhere that isn't anywhere. He looked at Mark.

"You don't believe me?" Mark said, stopping in his tracks and turning a full half circle so that he was facing him

"I don't know what to believe."

"Believe what I tell you."

"Yes, Sir," Tayler said with a grin, snapping to attention. Mark leaned over and the warm breath of his whisper taunted Tayler's neck. "I really mean it," he said.

"Time has a way of changing meaning," Tayler said with soft sadness in his voice. "And desire has a way of vanishing in time."

"Do you expect yours will?"

"I don't know."

They walked a little in silence until Tayler took Mark's hand. "Now it's my turn," he said, "to ask for forgiveness."

"For what?" Mark said, truly puzzled.

"For being a wet blanket."

"Wet as you are, I'd love to crawl under you. Come home with me. We can have some hot rum and you can fuck me. I'm starting to feel you inside me already." Tayler spotted a cab and hailed it. They sped through the city and got out in the urban pastoral of a snow-swept Washington Heights.

"I want it to be always like this," Mark said, his arm wrapped around Tayler's bare shoulder, looking into his eyes. Always."

Tayler nodded his head and smiled wistfully, fleetingly and then kissed Mark gently on the lips. He understood that he was committing himself to something that was sure to get out of his control.

If you enjoyed this sample then look for **Sweet Surrender.**

Also by this Author

A Second Chance

The Recruiter

A Furtive and Hidden Embrace

Diamond Shadows

Displacement

Keen Obedience

Between Two Thieves

Heart's Desire

Sensual Surrender

Erotic Aggression

Don't Forget You Love Me

Unstable Emotion

The Hazard Game

A Knight in the Forest

Captured Emotions

About the Author

Gideon Elliot was born on 1981 in Wichita, Kansas.

He grew up in San Francisco and spends the greater part of the year, now, on one of the Cyclades Islands in Greece where he runs a jazz café, paints, writes poetry, and swims.

He has a small apartment in Greenwich Village, where he stays from the middle of November to the end of April and, during those months, manages an erotic men's clothing shop.

He began writing erotic fiction at the age of fifteen.

From the Author

Check my page on Amazon and my blog for Updates and interesting info.

Author Central - http://www.amazon.com/Gideon-Elliot/e/B00DUYBEQC

If you enjoyed any of my books then please share the love and click like on my books in Amazon.

If you write me a review and send me an email I will send you a free book, or many.
(Just know that these emails are filtered by my publisher.)

Good news is always welcome.

One Last Thing, For Kindle Readers...

When you turn the page, Kindle will give you the opportunity to rate this book and share your thoughts on Facebook and Twitter. If you enjoyed my writings, would you please take a few seconds to let your friends know about it? Because... when they enjoy they will be grateful to you and so will I.

Thank You!

Gideon Elliot
gideon_elliot@awesomeauthors.org